For Michael and Jack and all of their
Texas-Tickling, Kansas-Crushing relatives

—C. C. J.

ALADDIN • An imprint of Simon & Schuster Children's Publishing Division • 1230 Avenue of the Americas, New York, New York 10020 • First Aladdin hardcover edition June 2018 • Text copyright © 2018 by Cindy Chambers Johnson • Illustrations copyright © 2018 by Daniel Duncan • All rights reserved, including the right of reproduction in whole or in part in any form. • ALADDIN and related logo are registered trademarks of Simon & Schuster, Inc. • For information about special discounts for bulk purchases, please contact Simon & Schuster Special Sales at 1-866-506-1949 or business@simonandschuster.com. • The Simon & Schuster Speakers Bureau can bring authors to your live event. For more information or to book an event contact the Simon & Schuster Speakers Bureau at 1-866-248-3049 or visit our website at www.simonspeakers.com. • Book designed by Laura Lyn DiSiena • The illustrations for this book were rendered digitally. • The text of this book was set in MrsEaves. • Manufactured in China 0318 SCP • 1 2 3 4 5 6 7 8 9 10 • Library of Congress Control Number 2017955448 • ISBN 978-1-4814-9159-4 (hc) • ISBN 978-1-4814-9160-0 (eBook)

RUSSELL WRESTLES *the* RELATIVES

By CINDY CHAMBERS JOHNSON

Illustrated by DANIEL DUNCAN

ALADDIN

New York London Toronto Sydney New Delhi

There was only one day left until Russell's family reunion. Everyone was excited.

Everyone except **Russell**.

Family reunions meant lots of hugging, hand shaking, and hair tousling.

And Russell's relatives? Well, they were a bit more . . .
enthusiastic than most.
They were BIGGER than most.
They were BRAWNIER than most.

They were **WRESTLERS**.

Russell's granddaddy was the Texas Tickler.

He'd been perfecting his famous Texas Ticklehold for the better part of a century.

The only wrestler who could beat him was Russell's grammy, Dorothy the Dropper, with her Kansas Crusher.

Every one of Russell's aunts, uncles, and cousins was a wrestler. They were sure to greet him with humongous hugs and Herculean handshakes.

Russell was small and scrawny.

He'd be squished like a toothpaste tube.

He had to do something to save himself.

He needed a plan.

Reunion day arrived faster than a two-second count. At the sound of the bell, Russell ran and hid in the laundry basket. He thought he was safe . . .

until Mom caught him in an ankle hold.
"What are you doing in there?"
She switched to a wrist lock.

"Hey, Russell!" His cousins Lorry and Tory, the Twin Tornados, tag-teamed him with back-to-back Backbusters.

Russell slid across the floor . . .

where Uncle "Iron Arm" Murphy
caught Russell's hand in his vise grip.
"Nice to see you, young man," he bellowed,
and gave Russell the
Earthquake Shake.

Russell vibrated from head to toe.

When Uncle Iron Arm finally released him, Russell

r-r-rumbled r-r-right

into the arms of his cousin Cora, The Cleaner.
She grabbed him in her Washing Machine hold.

When Cora started the Spin Cycle,
Russell thought he was a goner.
How could he run and hide if he
couldn't get away?

His belly flip-flopped. His head swam.
He gasped, and his stomach sucked in as skinny as a snake's.
Then, to his surprise . . .

he

slid

right

out

of Cora's grasp.

"Nice move," Lorry said.
"Move?" Russell asked, inching toward the plant stand.

"What's that called?" Tory asked.
"Um . . . the Slippery Sidewinder?"

Just then Uncle Louie the Loon advanced for a Tousle Tangler. When Russell saw that big hand coming at him, he ducked and covered his head.

"Hey, the Duck and Cover!" Uncle Louie said.

You're a fast thinker.

Who, me?

Russell was so astonished, he didn't notice Aunt Patty,
The Pincher, sneaking up until she lunged.

He wiggled like a worm
and saved his cheeks in
the nick of time.

Pretty soon he was making up
moves left and right.
The Jumping Bean was
excellent against Aunt Franny
the Flapper's Lindy Hop Bop.

Uncle "El Monstruo" Morty had to use Russell's Duck and Cover when Russell used the . . .

Twist and
SHOUT.

He even kept Granddaddy
and his Texas Ticklehold at
arm's length by moving in
with a Knuckle Knocker.

Russell puffed out his chest. "Who is Russell the Wrestler's next challenger?" he shouted, and backed right into . . .

Grammy Dorothy.

My sweet Russell!

She grabbed him in her Kansas Crusher.

Russell tried the
Slippery Sidewinder,
but Grammy hung on.

He used the Wiggle
Worm. Grammy
squeezed tighter.

Even the Twist and Shout
was no match for
Grammy's grip.
Russell was almost ready
to throw in the towel.

He rested his head on
Grammy's shoulder.
He was down for the
count . . . or was there
one more move
he could try?

Russell raised his chin.
He puckered his lips.
He planted a big wet smacker on
Grammy's cheek.

A grin spread across Grammy's face.

Her knees buckled.

She swooned.

Russell's smile was wider than
a championship belt.

Until . . .

HEY, WHERE'S MINE?

everybody wanted a Smackdown Smooch.

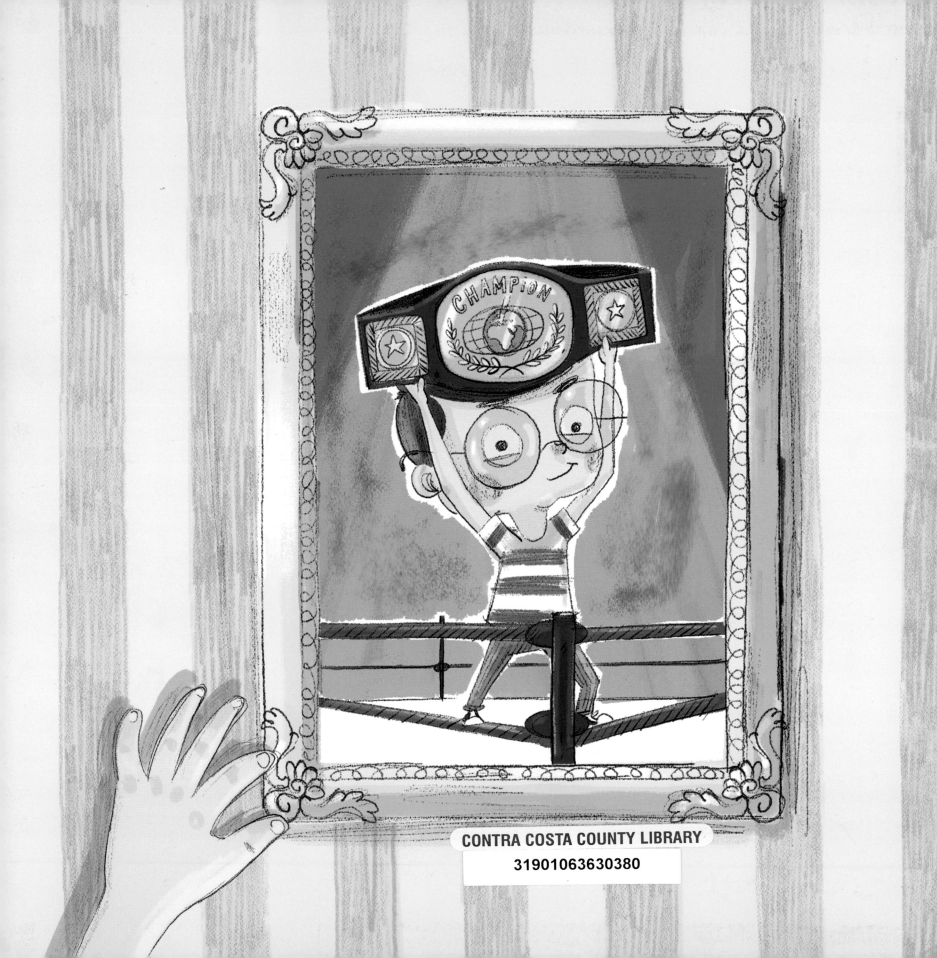